D0060461

big
NATE
I CAN'T TAKE IT!

Complete Your *Big Nate* Collection

big NATE
I CAN'T TAKE IT!

by LINCOLN PEIRCE

Andrews McMeel
PUBLISHING®

Big Nate is distributed internationally by Andrews McMeel Syndication.

Big Nate: I Can't Take It! copyright © 2013 by United Feature Syndicate, Inc. All rights reserved. Printed in China. No part of this book may be used or reproduced in any manner whatsoever without written permission except in the case of reprints in the context of reviews.

Andrews McMeel Publishing
a division of Andrews McMeel Universal
1130 Walnut Street, Kansas City, Missouri 64106

www.andrewsmcmeel.com

ISBN: 978-1-4494-2937-9

Library of Congress Control Number: 2013933500

Made by:
Shenzhen Donnelley Printing Company Ltd.
Address and location of manufacturer:
No. 47, Wuhe Nan Road, Bantian Ind. Zone,
Shenzhen China, 518129
Box Set 1st Printing—7/15/19

Big Nate can be viewed on the Internet at
www.gocomics.com/big_nate.

ATTENTION: SCHOOLS AND BUSINESSES
Andrews McMeel books are available at quantity discounts with bulk purchase for educational, business, or sales promotional use. For information, please e-mail the Andrews McMeel Publishing Special Sales Department:
specialsales@amuniversal.com.

ARRRRRRGH!
DANG!

WHAT'S UP, NATE?

I'M MAKING A SNOWMAN, BUT I CAN'T GET THIS SECOND SNOWBALL UP ON TOP OF THE FIRST ONE!

AH! WHAT WE HAVE HERE, SON, IS A **PHYSICS** PROBLEM!

A PIECE OF LUMBER FOR A LEVER, AND A CINDER BLOCK FOR A FULCRUM!...

THEN I'LL JUMP OFF THIS STEP-LADDER, AND MY WEIGHT WILL PROPEL THE SNOWBALL UPWARD!

WOW! PRETTY COOL, DAD!

✶AHEM!✶ I WAS AT THE TOP OF MY HIGH SCHOOL PHYSICS CLASS!

CHONK!

CRASH!

HOW'D YOU DO IN WOOD SHOP?

A SHLOX-TV *REALITY* special:
NEW YEAR'S EVE
with
ELLEN WRIGHT!

OUR HEROINE

with your hosts:
BIFF BIFFWELL   CHIP CHIPSON

It's December 31st, Chip, and typical teen ELLEN WRIGHT is preparing for...

...a ROCKIN' NEW YEAR'S PARTY!

DING DONG!

...And here's her date! Loyal yet hapless boyfriend GORDIE!

The poor sap.

We will now FOLLOW Ellen and Gordie to the party and provide a LIVE report from...

HOLD ON, Biff! Not so fast!

There'll be a slight delay! Ellen needs to...

← Dramatic pause

"FRESHEN UP"!

dismayed expression ↘

Why don't you handle the play by-play, Chip?

Right, Biff! She's reaching for the foundation...

Now the blush... the concealer... the rouge... the eyeshadow... the mascara...

EGAD! Will it NEVER END??

Hey, when you look like Ellen, you've got to go ALL OUT!

Good point, Biff.

ALMOST READY!

2001...

...A FACE ODYSSEY.

FETCH!

MR. EUSTIS? WHEN DID YOU GET SPITSY?

✻CHUCKLE!✻... I REMEMBER IT SO WELL!

I WAS OUT FOR A DRIVE ONE DAY WHEN I NOTICED A SIGN BY A FARMHOUSE!

"PUPPIES FOR SALE"

"IT WAS A LITTER OF SEVEN! THEY ALL LOOKED ABOUT THE SAME."

"...ALL EXCEPT **ONE**! RIGHT IN THE MIDDLE WAS A SPUNKY LITTLE FELLA WITH A LOT OF ENERGY!"

"HE WAS BIGGER AND FEISTIER THAN THE OTHERS! I COULDN'T TAKE MY EYES OFF HIM!"

SO THAT PUPPY WAS SPITSY, EH?

NO, **THAT** PUPPY WAS **TAKEN** ALREADY!

SPITSY WAS IN A CORNER WITH HIS HEAD STUCK IN A MILK CARTON!

IT'S ALL STARTING TO MAKE SENSE.

HI, BOY! NEED SOME HELP?

YOU'LL HAVE 45 MINUTES TO COMPLETE THIS TEST.

OKAY, HERE WE GO! NUMBER ONE!...

I'LL COME BACK TO THAT ONE.

NUMBER TWO...

UMM.... I'LL COME BACK TO THAT ONE, TOO.

NUMBER THREE... HEY, WHAT **IS** THIS? I HARDLY KNOW **ANY** OF THESE!

mumble

huh?

?

?

?

grumble

WHOOPS! MY APOLOGIES, PEOPLE! I GAVE YOU THE **WRONG TEST!**

I GAVE YOU THE TEST FOR MY **OTHER** CLASS! THEY'RE TWO CHAPTERS AHEAD OF YOU!

HERE'S THE **RIGHT** TEST!

AS I SAID, YOU HAVE 45 MINUTES.

OKAY! NUMBER ONE!

CAN I HAVE THE OTHER TEST BACK?

20

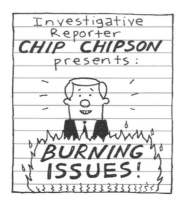

Investigative Reporter **CHIP CHIPSON** presents:

BURNING ISSUES!

Friends, today's "burning issue" is **BULLYING!** And here to discuss it is celebrity psychologist **DR. WARREN FUZZY!**

Chip, bullying is the scourge of our schools!

We all remember what it's like to be bullied! We've all felt **POWERLESS!**

...but what we **DON'T REALIZE** is how powerless the **BULLIES** feel!

The **BULLIES** feel powerless??

Right, Chip! That's why they're bullies!

They're **COMPENSATING** for their underlying sense of inadequacy! Underneath, they're **COWARDS!**

Once we know that, we can **STAND UP** to the bullies and **STOP** the cycle of bullying!

NATE.

HMM?

I'M WATCHING YOU, MISTER.

Does that really work?

Unless they're teachers. Then you just live in fear.

WHAT **HAP**PENED? MY BACK WENT OUT DURING THIRD PERIOD.

I'M IN AGONY.

I KNOW WHAT'LL HELP! GET ON THE FLOOR!

MY BROTHER-IN-LAW IS A CHIROPRACTOR! I SAW HIM DO THIS ONCE!

BY APPLYING PRESSURE TO THE RIGHT SPOT, I CAN SHIFT YOUR SPINE BACK INTO ALIGNMENT!

MMPH!

ARRGH!

EVER SEEN THE INSIDE OF THE TEACHERS' LOUNGE? NOPE.

GIVE YOU A BUCK IF YOU PEEK INSIDE!

YOU'RE ON!

A BUCK DOESN'T COMPENSATE ME FOR THE NIGHT-MARES I'LL BE HAVING ALL SUMMER.

NATE!

YIP!

WOULD YOU MIND EXPLAINING **WHY** YOU'RE BRINGING A **ROCK** INTO SCHOOL?!

IT'S A COUNTER-WEIGHT!

A COUNTER-WEIGHT.

SO I WON'T TIP OVER!

MY BACKPACK IS SO LOADED DOWN WITH HOMEWORK I CAN'T **WALK** NORMALLY!

"PSYCH-OUT" TIME!

 WELL, WELL! NUMBER 23!

 NUMBER 23 ON YOUR JERSEY... ON YOUR WRISTBAND... YOUR SOCKS... YOUR SNEAKERS...

 TRYING TO "BE LIKE MIKE", HUH? THAT'S SAD, MAN.

 SAD? YEAH. SORT OF PATHETIC, Y'KNOW?

 YOU'RE TRYING TO BE MICHAEL JORDAN! IT'S NOT GONNA HAPPEN! YOU HAVE **NO** CHANCE!

 MYSELF, I DON'T LIVE VICARIOUSLY THROUGH **OTHER** PEOPLE! I DON'T PATTERN MYSELF AFTER **ANYONE**!

 SO YOU'RE TRYING TO BE LIKE... NOBODY. EXACTLY. YOU'RE SUCCEEDING. NAB!

 I NEED TO WORK ON MY TRASH TALK. CAN YOU GO DO IT ON THE BENCH?

LOOKING AT OLD YEARBOOKS AGAIN?

YUP! THESE PHOTOS FROM FIFTEEN YEARS AGO ARE A **RIOT**!

HEE HEE! LOOK AT PRINCIPAL NICHOLS BACK THEN!

YEAH, I... HEL-**LO**! WHO'S **THIS**?

"MS. LESSARD, SOCIAL STUDIES"! YOWZA! SHE'S **HOT**!

ROWR! SHE'S **ATOMIC**!

WHY CAN'T **WE** HAVE A TEACHER WHO LOOKS LIKE THAT?

WHAT'S UP, GENTS?

LOOK WHO WAS TEACHING SOCIAL STUDIES HERE FIFTEEN YEARS AGO!

WHAT A FOX, EH?

THAT'S MRS. GODFREY.

"LESSARD" WAS HER NAME BEFORE SHE GOT MARRIED.

I'M GOING TO BE VERY, VERY, VERY, VERY, VERY, VERY, VERY, VERY, VERY, VERY, VERY SICK.

Uh-oh! Nate and Ellen Wright are fighting again! This looks like a job for...

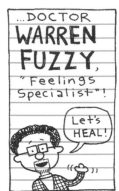
...DOCTOR **WARREN FUZZY**, "Feelings Specialist"!

Let's **HEAL**!

Kids! Accusations and anger are **NOT** the answer! Let's start a **DIALOGUE**!

Now sit down and **LOOK** at each other! **THAT'S** it!

Now, Nate... Tell Ellen: "When you _____, I feel _____."

But she...!

Tut TUT **TUT**! "When you _____, I feel _____."

When you act like a pinhead, I feel _like __ I'm going to _ hurl.

WONDERFUL! What have you learned about yourself?

That Ellen's a pinhead?

EXACTLY!

WHEN YOU DRAW INSULTING COMICS ABOUT ME, I FEEL LIKE WRINGING YOUR SCRAWNY LITTLE NECK.

!

WHAT'S UP, SON?

I'M ABOUT TO PLAY CHESS.

YOU ARE?

IN MY MIND. I'M GONNA PLAY A WHOLE MATCH MOVE BY MOVE.

YEAH, BUT...

SSH. IT'S STARTING.

DONE. CHECKMATE.

SNAP!

THAT DIDN'T TAKE LONG!

'COURSE NOT. I WAS PLAYING **YOU.**

AH.

WANNA PLAY CHESS?

WELL, NOW! LET'S CHECK OUT THE "TV GUIDE" AND SEE WHAT'S ON!

WE COULD WATCH THE HOCKEY GAME... OH, **NO** WE CAN'T! IT'S ON **CABLE**!

HERE'S A SHOW ABOUT THE GREAT PYRAMIDS! **OOPS! THAT'S** ON CABLE **TOO!**

SAY, HERE'S A GOOD MOVIE!... BUT **GUESS WHAT**?... IT'S ON **CABLE**!

GEE, I GUESS SITTING HERE READING THE TV GUIDE IS KIND OF **POINT**LESS, **ISN'T** IT, DAD?

YES

TRY READING THIS INSTEAD.

"GREAT EXPECTATIONS."

AND NO COMMERCIALS!

GUESS WHAT? I CAN PREDICT THE FUTURE!

SURE YOU CAN.

I **CAN!** I PREDICT MRS. GODFREY WILL TAKE TWO ASPIRIN DURING CLASS TODAY!

BET YOU A DOLLAR!

IT'S A BET!

RRINNG!

...AND ON JUNE 15TH, 1775, WHO WAS NAMED COMMANDER-IN-CHIEF?

NATE?

UH... I'M NOT SURE.

JUST TAKE AN EDUCATED GUESS, NATE.

I DUNNO. BEN FRANKLIN?

WELL, WE'VE HIT EVERY HOUSE IN THE NEIGHBORHOOD!

NOT **THIS** ONE!

THE O'MALLEYS?? DON'T WASTE YOUR TIME, NATE! THOSE OLD COOTS NEVER BUY **ANYTHING**!

FRANCIS, YOUR PROBLEM IS, YOU DON'T KNOW THE FIRST RULE OF SELLING!

WHAT'S THE FIRST RULE OF SELLING?

DING DONG!

GREETINGS, MRS. O'MALLEY! NATE WRIGHT HERE, OF JUNIOR WOODCHUCK TROOP 38!

I'M SELLING CALENDARS TODAY... BUT BEFORE YOU SAY **NO**, LET ME TELL YOU I'VE SET ASIDE **ONE** CALENDAR **ESPECIALLY** FOR YOU!

"TROPICAL BIRDS"... NO... "LOVE THOSE CATS"... NO... "CITY SKYLINES"...NO.... AH, **HERE** WE GO!

"FABIO 2001: SHIRTLESS AND SHAMELESS"!

I'LL TAKE IT!

"KNOW YOUR CLIENTELE"!

$ $

40

The Oddities Channel® presents...

"JOINED AT THE HIP: ENTWINED COUPLES"

Here's your host: BIFF BIFFWELL!

I'm speaking with Doctor LUKE WARM, the world's foremost authority on the phenomenon of ENTWINED COUPLES! Right, Doc?

Right, Biff!

Here we have a classic example! Fifteen-year-old ELLEN and her boyfriend GORDIE are VIRTUALLY INSEPARABLE!

You said "VIRTUALLY"! So they CAN be separated?

For brief periods, yes!

Observe: Ellen has to go use the bathroom! Look at the EFFORT it takes for her to break away!

While she's gone, Gordie is in ACUTE DISTRESS! He LITERALLY thinks he can't SURVIVE without her!

EXTREME CLOSE-UP!!

And now... LOOK! When she finally returns, their bond is RE-FORGED! STRONGER and CLOSER than EVER!

DID YOU MISS ME?

SURE DID.

GAG ME.

DAD, I HAVE TO DRAW A PORTRAIT OF SOMEONE FOR ART CLASS. WILL YOU SIT FOR ME?

WHY, SURE!

OKAY, WHY DON'T YOU SIT OVER HERE, AND I'LL...

NO, LET'S USE **THIS** CHAIR. IT HAS A NICER PATTERN.

NOW, LOOK STRAIGHT AHEAD AND...

ACTUALLY, WHY DON'T WE DO A THREE-QUARTERS VIEW? THAT WILL LOOK BETTER.

...AND LET'S TURN DOWN THE LIGHTS A BIT! IT'S TOO HARSH! TOO GLARING!

NATE, DON'T HOLD YOUR PAD IN YOUR LAP LIKE THAT! TILT IT UP SO YOU CAN **LOOK** AT ME WHILE YOU DRAW!

WHAT ARE YOU DOING? DON'T MOVE AROUND! THAT'LL CHANGE THE PERSPECTIVE! YOU'LL HAVE TO START OVER!

I'M DONE.

Hee Haw

Peirce

42

FOR MY ASSIGNMENT, I WAS SUPPOSED TO DO A REPORT ON THE "LINCOLN-DOUGLAS DEBATES".

BUT I COULDN'T! **WHY?** BECAUSE THERE **IS** NOBODY NAMED "LINCOLN DOUGLAS"!

BELIEVE ME, I **LOOKED!** I FOUND **PLENTY** OF DOUGLASES, BUT WERE ANY OF THEM **LINCOLN** DOUGLASES? **NO!**

...BUT HEY! LET'S SAY THERE **WAS** SOME TOTALLY OBSCURE GUY NAMED LINCOLN DOUGLAS! WHAT WERE THESE **DEBATES** ALL ABOUT? WHAT'S UP WITH **THAT?**

WHO WAS LINCOLN DOUGLAS DEBATING? WHEN DID IT HAPPEN? IF ANYBODY KNOWS, **TELL** ME, BECAUSE **I** CERTAINLY HAVE NO CLUE!

SO ANYWAY, YOU SEE MY PREDICAMENT! HOW CAN I WRITE A REPORT ON SOME CLOWN WHO NEVER **EXISTED?**

OBVIOUSLY, I **CAN'T!** SO INSTEAD, I DREW THIS GIANT QUESTION MARK TO FOREVER SYMBOLIZE THE UNKNOWABLE MYSTERY OF... LINCOLN DOUGLAS!

CLAP! CLAP! CLAP! CLAP! CLAP! CLAP! CLAP!

THANK YOU! THANK YOU!

CRIPES.

SHLOX-TV presents...

SURVIVE... OR ELSE!!

with your host: **KEN DOOLITTLE!!**

Here we are again, friends, in the **Social Studies classroom** where our intrepid survivors have been **TRAPPED** since early September!

They've had to endure countless hardships...

Have we **EVER!** Lectures, film strips, pop quizzes... Oh, the HORROR!

whimper

...And it's all because of MRS. GODFREY! She's making it IMPOSSIBLE to survive in here!

NATE - 6th grade tribe

Hmm... Sounds like you want to vote Mrs. Godfrey OUT of the classroom!

Oh, I **DO!**

So do I!

Me too!

And me!

Well, Mrs. Godfrey, the survivors have voted, and it looks like you're —

HOLD it, Ken. I didn't cast **MY** vote.

But...

No buts! What these "survivors" think is IRRELEVANT! I'm not going ANYWHERE!

I run this classroom, and I decide who stays and who goes!

46

LET'S DO THIS HOUSE NEXT.

WHOA! **HOLD** IT!

WHAT DO YOU GUYS THINK YOU'RE DOING?

SELLING WRAPPING PAPER, OBVIOUSLY.

NOT **HERE** YOU'RE NOT! YOU'RE FROM TROOP 22, RIGHT?

YEAH. SO?

THIS IS **TROOP 13** TERRITORY! THE RULE SAYS YOU CAN'T SELL STUFF IN ANOTHER TROOP'S NEIGHBORHOOD!

⚡SNORT!⚡ WE'LL SELL WRAPPING PAPER IN ANY NEIGHBORHOOD WE **WANT!**

I DON'T **THINK** SO.

URK!

DING DONG

WOULD YOU LIKE TO BUY SOME WRAPPING PAPER TO SUPPORT GOOD CITIZENSHIP THROUGH SCOUTING?

Time Once Again For...

"WHAT'S YOUR OCCUPATION"?

Here's your host: *BIFF BIFFWELL!*

Today, friends, I'm speaking to an actual ARTISTIC MUSE!

Right, Biff! I'm the official muse of P.S. 38 Art Teacher MR. ROSA!

What does an artistic muse **DO**, exactly?

I help him think up assignments! Those babies don't invent themSELVES!

Who do you think came up with the "linoleum print" project? Who created the "saran-wrap stained-glass-window" assignment? ME!

Very impressive!

BUT TIRING! Being that creative is EXHAUSTING!

Why don't you take a vacation?

And leave Mr. Rosa to think up projects HIMSELF? I don't know....

Oh, come on! You DESERVE it!

You know, you're RIGHT! For his next class, Mr. Rosa is ON HIS OWN!

"FREE DRAWING", PEOPLE.

LAME.

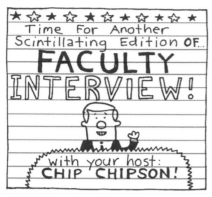

★☆★☆★☆★☆★
Time For Another Scintillating Edition OF...

FACULTY
INTERVIEW!

with your host:
CHIP CHIPSON!

Hello, friends! Today I'm chatting with P.S. 38's "Jabba the Hutt" look-alike... Social Studies teacher **MRS. GODFREY**!!

Can't talk now. I'm busy.

Ah! I see you're correcting **NATE WRIGHT's** most recent test!

That's right, Chip, and he is **FAILING** miserably!

And yet... you seem **HAPPY** about that!

Of **COURSE** I'm happy about it! That's what **I WANTED** to happen!

I... I don't understand.

I told Nate to study Chapter Three! **Then** I tested him on Chapter **TWELVE**!

But... that's totally **UNFAIR**!

Exactly! That's how he'll **LEARN**: by absorbing **DEFEAT** after devastating **DEFEAT**!

You've got to **BREAK** kids' **spirits** while they're young, Chip! Sure, it may seem cruel... but deep down they **LOVE** you for it!

OH, HOW I LOATHE HER.

JUST AN OBSERVATION: THERE WERE NO MATADORS AT THE BATTLE OF BULL RUN.

HI, MRS. SHIPULSKI! NATE "SCOOP" WRIGHT HERE FROM THE P.S. 38 WEEKLY BUGLE!

CAN I INTERVIEW PRINCIPAL NICHOLS?

HE'S IN HIS OFFICE WITH MS. BROWN RIGHT NOW.

OOOOOOH! MR. NICHOLS AND MS. BROWN! HUBBA **HUBBA**!

WAIT! WHAT ARE YOU DOING?

DON'T MAKE IT SOUND AS IF THERE'S SOMETHING **SLEAZY** GOING ON!

A MEETING BETWEEN A TEACHER AND THE PRINCIPAL ISN'T SOME **GOSSIP** ITEM! IT'S A SCHOOL AFFAIR!

AN **AFFAIR**! CAN I QUOTE YOU ON THAT? NO!

I DIDN'T MEAN IT **THAT** WAY! DON'T WRITE THAT! DON'T USE THE WORD "AFFAIR"!

OKAY, OKAY...

HOW DO YOU SPELL "TRYST"?

IS IT AN "I" OR A "Y"?

SIR, WE HAVE A "CODE RED" OUT HERE.

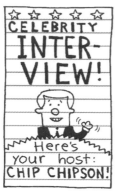

☆ ☆ ☆ ☆ ☆
CELEBRITY
**INTER-
VIEW!**

Here's
your host:
CHIP CHIPSON!

Friends, our
guest today
is "canine
control
specialist"
**HERMAN
SHEPHERD!**

Howdy,
Chip.

Herman, isn't
"canine control
specialist" just a
fancy-pants way
of saying
"**DOG CATCHER**"?

Not
at
all!

Of course, rounding up
strays is **PART** of it,
but the most **IMPORT-
ANT** aspect of the job
is **PROTECTING THE
PUBLIC!**

For example: in 1997 I
captured the infamous
"**HYDRO PHOEBE**" and her
rabid band of followers!

I also
collared
"Attila
the
Husky"
in 1999...

...and, in
2001,
"Notorious
P.U.G!"

Impressive
resumé!

Believe
me, Chip,
they're
not **ALL**
success
stories. **MANY**
dogs have
slipped through
my fingers!

Not **HARDENED
CRIMINALS**, mind
you, but dogs
who nonetheless
are **DANGEROUS!**
Dogs who are a
MENACE to every-
one around them!

DID YOU
HEAR
SOME-
THING?

HM?

Peirce

COACH! WHAT ARE WE DOING TODAY?

JUGGLING OR SQUARE DANCING! YOUR CHOICE!

⁂SPUTTER!⁂ JUGGLING? SQUARE DANCING?

UH HUH.

BUT THOSE AREN'T EVEN SPORTS!

THEY'RE PART OF THE PHYS. ED. CURRICULUM.

CURRICULUM SHMURRICULUM!! WHAT DOES SQUARE DANCING HAVE TO DO WITH ANYTHING??

HOW ABOUT A GOOD OLD-FASHIONED GAME OF "BOMBARDMENT"? OR SOME FLOOR HOCKEY? HUH? HOW 'BOUT IT?

ISN'T THE WHOLE POINT OF PHYS. ED. TO BREAK A SWEAT?

ABSO-LUTELY.

FIFTY MORE, THEN MOP UP THAT PUDDLE.

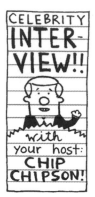

CELEBRITY **INTER-VIEW!!**

with your host: **CHIP CHIPSON!**

Folks, I'm coming to you live from **HEAVEN** where I'm chatting with legendary commander-in-chief... **ABE LINCOLN!**

So, Abe... excited about tomorrow?

Tomorrow?

PRESIDENTS' DAY! It's your birthday celebration!

Actually, Chip, my birthday was **LAST** week.

Tomorrow is simply an excuse to sell cars and have a three-day weekend.

But hey, what can I tell you? I get no respect!.. ...not even from my fellow **ex-presidents** around here!

Like **WASHINGTON** over there! He's always busting my chops because **HIS** face is on the **QUARTER** and **MY** face is only on the...

HEY, ABE! "PENNY" FOR YOUR THOUGHTS!

WAHA HA HA HA HA Good HA one, George! HA HA HA HA HA

Happy Presidents' Day!

OH, YEAH? NICE TEETH!

KLASSIC KOMIX
← OPEN

NATE!

HI, GORDIE. UM...IS IT OKAY IF I HANG OUT HERE?

SURE! WHY **WOULDN'T** IT BE OKAY?

WELL...I JUST WONDERED... BECAUSE OF YOU AND ELLEN...

NATE, YOUR SISTER AND I MAY HAVE BROKEN UP, BUT THAT DOESN'T CHANGE ANYTHING BETWEEN **US!**

REALLY? SO I CAN STILL COME BY TO TALK WITH YOU ABOUT COMICS?

OF COURSE!

AND CAN I STILL HELP YOU WHEN YOU TAKE INVENTORY?

ABSOLUTELY!

AND...

NATE, YOU'LL **ALWAYS** BE WELCOME AT "KLASSIC KOMIX"!

YOU'RE AMONG FRIENDS HERE!

WE NEED A TEACHER PROFILE FOR OUR NEXT EDITION. NATE, DO AN INTERVIEW WITH MR. GALVIN.

WHAT? WHOA!

HOW COME **I'VE** ALWAYS GOT TO DO THE LAME TEACHER INTERVIEWS?

JUST BECAUSE **YOU'RE** THE EDITOR, GINA, THAT DOESN'T MEAN YOU CAN MAKE **ME** DO ALL THE **GRUNT** WORK!

YOU INTERVIEW MR. GALVIN! GIVE **ME** SOMETHING **ELSE** TO DO!

✷ SIGH... ✷

OKAY! STOP WHINING! **I'LL** DO THE PIECE ON MR. GALVIN!

YOU CAN DO THE "UP CLOSE AND PERSONAL" WITH DEBBI DALTON.

WHO'S DEBBI DALTON?

SHE'S AN EIGHTH-GRADE GIRL WHO'S TRYING TO GET PERMISSION TO JOIN THE BOYS' WRESTLING TEAM.

...SO THEN I WROTE **ANOTHER** PETITION...

MY PENCIL JUST BROKE.

Peirce

BIFF BIFFWELL'S

WORLD OF **DISCOVERY!**

Friends, have YOU ever wondered what happens to a DAY... once it's OVER?

I know I have!

So we've come to the "Island of Used-Up Days" to speak with YESTERDAY: MARCH 23rd!

So... how'd things go for you yesterday?

I'll be honest with you, Biff: it was pretty dull.

But there's always next year.

Next year?

That's how the "Island of Used-Up Days" works, Biff. I'll hang out here for the next 364 days until it's my turn again!

There's always hope that NEXT year, I'll be a historically significant day!

Hmm... Has that happened to you in the past?

Well... not really.

On March 23rd, 1912, the Dixie Cup was invented...

And on March 23rd, 1985, piano man Billy Joel married supermodel Christie Brinkley....

...but... ※sigh※ I'm just not one of the "big guys."

23rd! What's up?

WHACK!

Who was that?

July 4th. Lucky stiff.

READY... BEGIN.

For each problem in this section, there are five suggested answers. Show your work in the space at the right of the page. Then select which of the five choices is correct.

1. Tom, Dick and Harry are members of the same scout troop and are collecting merit badges. There are 28 merit badges available, divided equally into two types: silver and gold.

Tom has collected 25% of the available merit badges; one of them is gold. Dick has collected 50% of the available merit badges; three of them are silver. Harry has collected 75% of the available merit badges; eleven of them are gold.

Harry has collected all the merit badges that Tom has. He has also collected the same gold merit badges that Dick has. But Harry has not collected any of the silver merit badges that Dick has.

Assuming that Tom and Dick do not earn any more merit badges, how many more merit badges must Harry earn to guarantee that he will have the same silver badges (hint: but not necessarily the same NUMBER of badges) as Dick?

RRRRIINNNGGG

NOT ONLY DO I NEED A MATH TUTOR, I MAY ALSO HAVE TO INVEST IN A SPEED-READING COURSE.

☆★☆★☆
Celebrity
**INTER-
VIEW!**

with:
*BIFF
BIFFWELL!*

Today, friends, we're chatting with the "month of the month"... MARCH!

Hi, Biff.

So, March... "In like a lion, Out like a lamb," eh?

Yeah. Like I've never heard THAT before.

Now, now, li'l feller. No need to be snippy about it.

Hey... HEY! Don't patronize me!

PAT PAT!

I know what you're thinking, Biff: "Oooh, he's a LAMB! SPRING is here!"

Well, Spring isn't here YET, folks! And I've still got plenty of LION left in me!

But... but you look so DOCILE!

⁂sigh...⁂ Okay, you want proof? I'll give you proof.

RROARR

66

SHLOX-TV presents: "ARE U A STAR?" with your host: TY DYSON!

Hi, friends! Did you ever wonder where the next **Britney Spears** or **Nsync** will come from? Well, **WE** did!

So we're searching the country, asking the young people: ARE U A STAR?

I'M a star, Ty!

Well now! What's your name?

I'm **ELLEN WRIGHT**. I'm 15 years old, and I AM A STAR!

Great! What's your talent?

Talent?

What MAKES you a star, Ellen? Do you sing? Do you dance?

Um... I just want to be famous.

For doing **WHAT**?

Whatever. I'll do anything!

I'm sorry, Ellen. U ARE **NOT** A STAR!

I... I'm not?

SPRING TRAINING

BATTER UP!

THE CRACK OF THE BAT

ROUNDING FIRST...

RIBBA
DRIBBA
DRIBBA
DRIBBA
DRIBBA
IBBA
RIBBA
DRIBBA
IBBA

IF I MAKE THIS, IT MEANS I'M GONNA ACE THE SOCIAL STUDIES EXAM TOMORROW!

FOOSH!

YEAH, BABY!

SWISH! AN A-PLUS IS IN THE **BAG!**

WELL, IN THAT CASE...

WHEN AND WHERE DID CORNWALLIS SURRENDER?

OKAY, IF I MAKE **THIS** ONE, IT MEANS THERE WON'T BE ANY CORNWALLIS QUESTIONS ON THE EXAM!

SWISH!

YES!

※ SIGH... ※

Peirce

HERE, NATE. PLEASE TAKE THIS OVER TO THE NELSONS' HOUSE.

A **DOLL**?

IT'S ONE OF ELLEN'S OLD ONES. I TOLD MRS. NELSON SHE COULD HAVE IT FOR HER DAUGHTER.

✳ SPUT!... ✳ I CAN'T BE SEEN WALKING AROUND WITH **THIS** THING!

I'LL TAKE IT OVER THERE **UNDER COVER**!

WHATEVER.

HEY, WRIGHT.

HEY, WHAT'S WITH THE BACKPACK, WRIGHT? GOING TO SUMMER SCHOOL?

OoooOH! **SUM**MER SCHOOL!

I'M **NOT** GOING TO SUMMER SCHOOL! I'M DOING AN ERRAND!

WHAT ERRAND?

UH... WELL... IT'S...

YOU **ARE** GOING TO SUMMER SCHOOL! WHAT'S IN HERE, YOUR **HOMEWORK**?

HEY! DON'T TOUCH THAT!

OKAY, OKAY! YOU DON'T HAVE TO **CRY** ABOUT IT!

WAAH! WAAH! I NEED A DIAPER CHANGE!

WOULD IT HAVE KILLED YOU TO REMOVE THE BATTERIES?

I'M 0-FOR-3 AGAINST THIS PITCHER. HE'S GOT MY NUMBER.

POSITIVE VISUAL-IZATION.

HUH?

IN YOUR MIND, PICTURE YOURSELF SUCCEEDING! THEN IT'LL HAPPEN!

KRAK!

CAUTION! OPEN SEWER

STRIKE THREE!!

?!?

AAAH, **SPRING!** WHAT A DAY!

SI'I'I'I'IGH....

WOOF!

HMM? OH, YOU WANT ME TO THROW THAT BALL, SPITSY? OKAY... JUST ONCE!

GO GET IT!!

I SAID GO **GET** IT, SPITSY!

PANT PANT PANT PANT PANT

GOOD GRAVY. YOU REALLY **ARE** CLUELESS, AREN'T YOU?

PANT PANT PANT PANT PANT

FINE! I'LL GET IT MY**SELF!**

A DOG WHO DOESN'T KNOW HOW TO FETCH! NATE'S RIGHT ABOUT YOU, SPITSY!

HE'S ALWAYS SAYING YOU'RE THE DUMBEST DOG HE'S EVER...

!!

AAAAAAHHHH....

SPRING IS HERE! THE SNOW IS GONE! WHAT'S THAT GREEN STUFF? IT'S OUR LAWN!

OUR COATS AND HATS WE'VE TOSSED ASIDE! LET'S GRAB OUR BIKES AND TAKE A RIDE!

WE'LL PLAY SOME CATCH! WE'LL TOSS SOME 'BEES! WE'LL SWING SOME BATS! THE DAY WE'LL SEIZE!

VERY POETIC.

I WROTE IT MYSELF! IT'S CALLED "ODE TO SPRING"!

NOW **I'VE** GOT SOMETHING TO READ.

"I.O.U. ONE FULL DAY OF WORK. ACTUAL DATE AND DETAILS TO BE DETERMINED BY DAD."

YOU WROTE THAT BACK IN JANUARY.

✧SIGH...✧

"OWED TO SPRING."

HEADS UP!

HUH?

OW!

BONK!

THANKS A **LOT**, FRANCIS!

HEY, I SAID HEADS UP!

EXACTLY! YOU SAID HEADS UP! SO I LOOKED **UP!**

SO?

SO IT WAS A **GROUND BALL**, FOOL!

WELL, WHAT AM I **SUPPOSED** TO SAY? "HEADS **DOWN**"?

SAY **ANY**THING! ANYTHING THAT MAKES **SENSE!**

HOW ABOUT THIS: LOOK OUT!

GOOD! MUCH BETTER!

LOOK OUT! **LOOK OUT!**

LOOK OUT!

O**KAY**, FRANCIS! YOU'VE MADE YOUR POINT! YOU DON'T HAVE TO...

84

LITTLE LEAGUE ROSTERS TODAY

PICK UP UNIFORMS HERE

HI, COACH!

WELL! HELLO, GENTS! READY FOR ANOTHER GREAT SEASON?

T-BALL
DOUBLE A
MAJORS

COACH

UH... THAT DEPENDS ON OUR TEAM NAME.

YEAH, WHO'S OUR SPONSOR?

...BECAUSE LAST YEAR WE PLAYED FOR A BEAUTY PARLOR! AND IT WAS MISSPELLED ON OUR UNIFORMS!

YEAH! "CHEEZ LINDA"! WE WERE A LAUGHING-STOCK!

NOT TO WORRY, BOYS! "CHEEZ LINDA" IS NO MORE!

REALLY?

WE HAVE A NEW SPONSOR?

WE CERTAINLY DO! AND THE NAME ISN'T MISSPELLED, EITHER!

COACH

Peirce

...UNFORTUNATELY.

NO!... NO!

CONTINUED NEXT WEEK!!

THIS IS **HORRIBLE!**

WHAT A **DISASTER!**

WHAT'S A DISASTER?

OUR TEAM NAME! **AGAIN!**

I DON'T BELIEVE THIS.

WHAT? WE'RE STILL "CHEEZ LINDA"?

WORSE.

MUCH WORSE.

WELL, **TELL** ME!

I CAN'T BRING MYSELF TO SAY IT OUT LOUD.

OH, FOR... FINE, I'LL JUST CHECK THE ROSTERS!

OKAY, SO OUR SPONSOR **IS...**

...THE BIGELOW MAT COMPANY?

LET'S GO, DOORMATS.

IT'S GOING TO BE A LONG SEASON.

KRAK!

HOME! HOME!! PLAY AT THE PLATE!

WUMP!

HOLY SMOKES! THIS GUY'S COMIN' FAST!... AND HE'S **HUGE!**

I'M GONNA GET FLATTENED LIKE A PANCAKE!

AND FOR **WHAT**? TO PREVENT A RUN IN A **LITTLE LEAGUE** GAME WE'RE ALREADY LOSING **TEN-ZIP**? IS IT REALLY WORTH IT?

I DON'T THINK SO.

SAFE!

HEY, STAN! YOU FORGOT TO WIPE YOUR FEET!

HA HA HA HA HA HA

PLAYING FOR THE "DOORMATS" IS BECOMING A SELF-FULFILLING PROPHECY.

Time Once Again For:

UP-CLOSE

★ AND ★

PERSONAL!

With your host: BIFF BIFFWELL!

Friends, today my special guest is "yearbook inscription expert" **ALAN ANNUAL!**

"Warm regards, Biff!"

Alan, what IS a "yearbook inscription expert"?

Biff, we've ALL been asked to sign yearbooks for classmates or teachers!

✦ Chuckle! ✦ So true! But we don't always know **WHAT TO WRITE!** That's where **I** come in!

I help folks find JUST THE RIGHT WORDS for a PAL...

See you this summer, ol' buddy ol' pal!

... or merely an **ACQUAINTANCE!**

Have a nice summer.

The object of one's affection...

Roses are red
Violets are great
Dump that jerk Ronnie
And go out with Nate!

... or perhaps a respected mentor!

Thou "ART" a great teacher! (Ha Ha!)

But Alan...what if you find yourself signing the yearbook of someone you **HATE?**

It **CAN** be done, Biff!

The trick is finding the perfect phrase! There truly **IS** an inscription for every occasion!

Mrs. Godfrey—I can't tell you how much I enjoyed your class this year.
Nate

Biff & Chip "ON SAFARI"

Greetings, friends! We're here in the wilds of Suburbia...

...to observe one of nature's most LOATHSOME creatures:

...the SIXTH-GRADE SOCIAL STUDIES TEACHER!

There she is, Biff! But... who's that WITH her?

That's a common schoolchild: "Academius Downtroddenus."

He looks EXHAUST-ED, Biff!

Oh, he IS! He's been her PRISONER since September!

SEPTEMBER? EGAD! Why doesn't she just EAT him and be DONE with it?

The schoolchild isn't FOOD for her, Chip! He's her AMUSEMENT! She screams at him, bosses him around, and brainwashes him with USELESS TRIVIA!

But... that's so CRUEL!

There IS hope, though, Chip. NATURE'S TIMETABLE is taking over!

See? She's going into SUMMER HIBERNATION!

...And "Academius Downtroddenus" can ESCAPE! RUN! RUN!

RRRRIINNNGG

sigh...

KRAK!

YES!

BAG OF CHIPS AND AN ORANGE SODA, PLEASE.

THE MOST EXCITING PLAY IN BASEBALL:

A FOUL BALL THAT LANDS NEAR THE SNACK BOOTH!

93

SNICKER! FRANCIS! TWO O'CLOCK!

HM?

IT'S ONLY TWELVE-THIRTY!

NO, NO! **LOOK** AT TWO O'CLOCK!

WHATTA YA MEAN, **LOOK** AT TWO O'CLOCK?

HAVEN'T YOU EVER SEEN A **WAR MOVIE**? IT'S A **DIRECTIONAL** THING!

TWELVE O'CLOCK IS STRAIGHT AHEAD! SIX O'CLOCK IS DIRECTLY BEHIND!

AND SO **TWO** O'CLOCK IS...

WAIT, WAIT! WHY WOULD SIX O'CLOCK BE **BEHIND** YOU?

I MEAN, WOULDN'T IT BE STRAIGHT DOWN?

NO, IT WOULD... YOU DON'T... OKAY, FOR**GET** IT! FORGET THE WHOLE CLOCK THING!

ALL I WAS **TRYING** TO SAY WITHOUT BEING **OBVIOUS** ABOUT IT WAS THAT THERE'S A DOOFUS IN A DORKY-LOOKING BATHING SUIT AHEAD AND TO THE RIGHT!

!

HE CLOCKED YOU!

TIME FOR AN ICE PACK.

WHAT THE-?

HEY, GUYS! CHECK OUT NATE AND FRANCIS!

THEY'RE PLAYING WITH **DOLLS**!

HA HA HA HA

SO?

YOU **ADMIT** IT?

SURE. WE'RE PLAYING WITH DOLLS.

'SCUSE ME.

FOOM!

CAN **WE** PLAY?

A MOMENT OF SILENCE, PLEASE, FOR "MALIBU BARBIE."

MAN! IT'S **BOILING** OUT HERE!

WHAT WAS I **THINKING**, WEAR-ING A **LONG-SLEEVE** UNDERSHIRT?

I'VE GOT TO GET THIS THING OFF BEFORE I GET **HEAT STROKE!**

BUT **HOW**? I CAN'T STRIP TO THE WAIST IN THE MIDDLE OF **RIGHT FIELD!**

WAIT! I'LL BET I CAN GET OUT OF THE UNDER-SHIRT **WITHOUT** TAKING OFF MY **UNIFORM!**

JUST GOTTA GET MY ARMS INSIDE HERE...

NOW GET MY HANDS FREE...

...AND PULL THIS OUT...

YES! DID IT!

THUD!

WONDER WHAT COACH IS YELLING ABOUT.

THERE!

PHYSICAL FITNESS MERIT BADGE, HERE I COME!

YOU'RE MY WITNESS, OKAY, FRANCIS? YOU'LL ATTEST TO THE FACT THAT I CLIMBED A FIFTEEN-FOOT ROPE!

YUP!

UP I GO!

YOU'RE HALFWAY!

OOF! GRUNT!

ALMOST THERE!

HM?

"(( ))" FWIP! FWIP!

YAAAH!

HOW'RE YOU DOING ON YOUR KNOT-TYING MERIT BADGE?

OW

HI, MISTER, I'M RAISING MONEY FOR MY LITTLE LEAGUE TEAM AND I...

WELL! LITTLE LEAGUE BASEBALL!

WHAT'S THE NAME OF YOUR TEAM? LET'S SEE HERE...

UH... WELL, IT'S..

DOES THAT SAY... "CHEEZ LINDA"?

YES

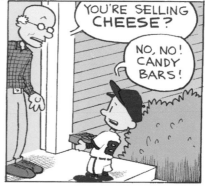

YOU'RE SELLING CHEESE?

NO, NO! CANDY BARS!

AH! BUT YOUR TEAM IS SPONSORED BY A CHEESE COMPANY!

NO, I... IT'S A MISTAKE ON OUR UNIFORMS! IT'S NOT SUPPOSED TO SAY THAT!

NOT SUPPOSED TO SAY WHAT?

THEY SPELLED IT WRONG! THEY SPELLED IT C-H-E-E-Z!

AND OF COURSE IT SHOULD BE C-H-E-E-S-E!

BUT WHO'S THIS LINDA?

RATHER THAN EXPLAIN THAT "CHEZ LINDA" IS A BEAUTY PARLOR, I JUST WALKED AWAY.

HI, NATE.

DARRYL! WHAT'S UP?

JUST ON MY WAY TO LAX PRACTICE.

LAX?? AREN'T YOU PLAYING BASEBALL THIS YEAR?

LAX IS MORE FUN. MY DAD DOESN'T KNOW ANYTHING ABOUT LAX.

WHATTA YA MEAN?

MY DAD USED TO BE AN AWESOME BASEBALL PLAYER. HE EVEN PLAYED THREE SEASONS IN THE MINOR LEAGUES.

SO HE'S, LIKE... MISTER BASEBALL SUPERSTAR?

RIGHT. AND HE WANTS ME TO BE AS GOOD AS **HE** WAS!

HE'S PRETTY INTENSE ABOUT IT. IT'S NO FUN HAVING A DAD WHO'S SUCH AN ATHLETE, I'LL TELL YOU.

I DON'T HAVE THAT PROBLEM. MY DAD'S A SPAZ.

☼ SIGH... ☼

YOU'RE LUCKY, DUDE.

I MEAN, A **TOTAL** SPAZ!

Peirce

HEY, WANT A FORTUNE COOKIE?

A FORTUNE COOKIE?

YEAH, WE WENT OUT FOR CHINESE FOOD LAST NIGHT!

THANKS.

"YOU SOMETIMES FAIL TO SEE THE FOREST FOR THE TREES."

✳SPUTTER!✳ WHAT KIND OF FORTUNE IS **THAT**? **THAT'S** NO **FORTUNE**!

A FORTUNE IS SUPPOSED TO TELL THE **FUTURE**! THIS IS JUST SOME LAME **SLOGAN**!

IF YOU'RE GOING TO CALL 'EM **FORTUNE** COOKIES, PUT AN ACTUAL **FORTUNE** IN 'EM!

DON'T TELL ME "YOU CAN'T SEE THE FOREST FOR THE TREES"! TELL ME WHAT'S GOING TO **HAPPEN**!!

WAM!

HOW PAIN-FULLY IRONIC.

IT SHOULD HAVE SAID "THE FOREST **OR** THE TREES"!

HERE COMES THAT NEW GIRL.

OOH! LET'S TALK TO HER!

GOOD LUCK. SHE WON'T TALK TO ANYONE. SHE SEEMS KIND OF STUCK-UP.

I'LL BET SHE'S JUST **SHY!** SHE DOESN'T TALK TO ANYONE BECAUSE NOBODY TALKS TO **HER!**

AND THERE'S NOTHING LIKE A **DOG** TO GET A CONVERSATION GOING!

SPITSY GOES UP TO HER, WAGS HIS TAIL... THEN **I** SWOOP IN AND CHARM HER **SOCKS OFF!**

WAG WAG WAG WAG WAG

GOT THAT, SPITSY? GO GET HER! GO SAY HI!

WHAT'S HAPPEN-ING?

CAN'T TELL. THERE'S A TREE IN THE WAY.

...BUT THAT'S ENOUGH TIME. I'M **GOIN' IN!**

HEL-LO!

IS THIS YOUR DOG?

WELL... PRACTICALLY. I DOG-SIT FOR HIM, YOU SEE, AND...

HE JUST **THREW UP ON MY FEET!**

AS PROMISED, HER SOCKS ARE OFF.

YOU SPAZ.

$"Money Matters" $ $
with your host
BIFF BIFFWELL
and special guest...

CONSUMER REPORTER
CELINE PAYCHEK!!

Hi, Celine!

Nice to be here, Biff!

Celine, it's BACK-TO-SCHOOL time again! Any shopping tips for parents trying to save a few pennies?

Absolutely, Biff!

DON'T be fooled by all the so-called "SALES"! That's the stuff the stores WANT you to buy!

Instead, check out the items marked "CLEARANCE"!

Your 11-year-old son might want a backpack like everyone ELSE's, but WHY PAY MORE?

Here's a perfectly good "Pinky the Pony" pack for HALF THE COST!

...And Biff, who needs some fancy-pants NOTE-BOOK with all those pockets, compartments, and zippers?

This plain brown binder is a STEAL, and the water damage is MINIMAL!

Then, of course, there's the matter of CLOTHES! Your children might beg you for "NICE" clothes that "FIT" and "LOOK GOOD"! ...AND, might I add, cost an ARM and a LEG!

Why pay through the nose? What's more important: some pair of pants your kid's going to outgrow... OR SAVING YOUR PRECIOUS, HARD-EARNED MONEY??

WE'LL TAKE 'EM!

SIGH...

CLEARAN

"CURIOSITY KILLED THE CAT."

DID YOU EVER REALLY **THINK** ABOUT THAT EXPRESSION, FRANCIS?

NOT REALLY.

LET'S ANALYZE IT: THE CAT DIED, RIGHT? **WHY** DID THE CAT DIE?

BECAUSE IT WAS TOO **STUPID** TO SEE WHAT WAS GOING ON!

NO, IT DIED BECAUSE IT WAS **CURIOUS!**

HIS KEEN, SEARCHING FELINE MIND GOT HIM INTO TROUBLE!

AH **HA!** TROUBLE HE WAS TOO **CLUELESS** TO GET **OUT** OF!

AND I SUPPOSE YOUR POINT IS THAT **DOGS** ARE SMARTER?

OF **COURSE** DOGS ARE SMARTER! A **DOG** WOULD NEVER...

YOU WERE SAYING?

YOU DUMB MUTT.

I JUST REMEMBERED YET **ANOTHER** EXPRESSION THAT **PROVES** DOGS ARE BETTER THAN CATS!

NOT THIS AGAIN.

"EVERY DOG HAS HIS DAY"! HOW 'BOUT **THAT**, HUH?

YEAH... SO?

SO YOU DON'T HEAR ANYBODY SAYING "EVERY **CAT** HAS HIS DAY," **DO** YOU?

NO! BECAUSE NOBODY **CARES** ABOUT CATS, THAT'S WHY!

BUT **DOGS**! DOGS **DESERVE** SOMETHING **GOOD**! HENCE: EVERY DOG HAS HIS DAY!

JUST ONE DAY, EH?

INTERESTING. **CATS** GET NINE WHOLE **LIVES**...

...BUT **DOGS** ONLY GET ONE PUNY LITTLE **DAY**!

DON'T WASTE IT!!

HEY, WRIGHT.

OH, HEY GUYS.

WHAT'S UP WITH YOUR **COACH**?

WHATTA YA MEAN?

HE'S WEARING A **UNIFORM**!

✻SNICKER!✻

WHAT DOES HE THINK THIS IS, MAJOR LEAGUE BASEBALL?

YEAH, WHO'S HE TRYING TO BE? JOE TORRE?

HE MUST BE ONE OF THOSE GROWN-UPS WHO THINKS HE CAN STILL **PLAY**!

HOW LAME CAN YOU GET?

HA HA

HA

HA HA HA

THAT'S NOT OUR COACH. THAT'S OUR PITCHER.

SECURITY IS HAVING A LITTLE LEAGUE STOPPER WITH FIVE O'CLOCK SHADOW.

I'VE **GOT** IT! **PROOF POSITIVE** THAT DOGS ARE BETTER THAN CATS!

AGAIN?

SEE THIS BOOK? IT'S ALL ABOUT **DOGS** THAT WERE **HEROES** IN **WARS**!

CANINE COURAGE

LOOK! DOGS THAT DELIVERED MESSAGES BEHIND ENEMY LINES! DOGS THAT RESCUED WOUNDED SOLDIERS! DOGS THAT SNIFFED OUT BOOBY TRAPS AND LAND MINES!

THAT SAYS IT ALL, FRANCIS! DOGS HAVE ANSWERED THE CALL IN THE HEAT OF **BATTLE**!

✳CHUCKLE!✳ HOW DO YOU THINK **PICKLES** HERE WOULD DO IN A **WAR**?

FSSSSST!

RROWR!!

I THINK SHE'D HAVE HER OWN REGIMENT!

I HATE CATS.

THERE'S NOTHING TO DO.

YOU SAID IT.

WHY DON'T YOU BOYS HIT ROCKS?

HIT ROCKS?

WITH A BAT! JUST KNOCK 'EM INTO THE TREES THERE!

WE USED TO DO THIS FOR **HOURS!**

WE WENT THROUGH A LOT OF BATS, I'LL TELL YOU!

'COURSE, BATS WERE **WOOD** BACK THEN!

OH, YEAH! GOT ALL OF **THAT** ONE!

SEE, GUYS? IT'S **FUN!**

YUP! THERE'S NOTHING QUITE LIKE HITTING ROCKS!

HA HA HA HA HA HA HA HA HA HA HA HA HA

HITTING **ROCKS!** GREAT IDEA, DAD!

YEAH! EXCITEMENT **PLUS!**

ROCK ON.

127

"EXTREME" SPORTS ARE THE WAVE OF THE FUTURE, RIGHT?

I GUESS.

HALF-PIPE, STREET LUGE, BUNGEE JUMPING... TWENTY YEARS AGO, NOBODY HAD EVEN **HEARD** OF THIS STUFF!

...SO **I** FIGURED: WHY NOT INVENT A **NEW** EXTREME SPORT?

ROLLER-VAULTING!

THAT LOOKS DANGEROUS.

OF **COURSE** IT'S DANGEROUS!

THAT'S WHY IT'S A SURE-FIRE **SUCCESS!** ...AND AS THE IN**VENTOR** OF THE SPORT, **I'LL** BE ITS FIRST **SUPERSTAR!**

BEFORE YOU KNOW IT, YOU'LL BE SEEING ME ON **TV!**

A LOCAL BOY IS LUCKY TO BE ALIVE TODAY AFTER HE...

THERE YOU ARE!

Peirce

MR. EUSTIS! I'VE FINALLY GOT THE COOKIES YOU ORDERED!

OH, DEAR.

OH, DEAR?

I'M ON A DIET.

I MEAN... I WASN'T ON A DIET WHEN I **ORDERED** THEM! BUT I AM **NOW**!

WELL...YOU **PAID** FOR 'EM! MIGHT AS WELL **TAKE** 'EM!

NO, NO... I COULDN'T.

IF I TAKE 'EM, THEY'LL LAST ABOUT ONE MINUTE! I'LL EAT 'EM! MY DIET WILL BE HISTORY!

GIVE 'EM TO SOMEBODY WHO REALLY **WANTS** 'EM!

I'M SKIPPING SUPPER TONIGHT.

WHAT'S UP, NATE?

WHOA! **WHOA!** KEEP THAT CAT AWAY FROM ME!

YOU KNOW I HATE CATS!

YOU'RE **AFRAID** OF 'EM, YOU MEAN!

I AM **NOT!** I JUST THINK THEY'RE USELESS, THAT'S ALL!

USELESS?

EX**ACT**LY! CATS ARE THE **OPPOSITE** OF **DOGS!**

DOGS **DO** STUFF! SLED DOGS! SEEING-EYE DOGS! RESCUE DOGS! SHEEP DOGS! DOGS ARE **USEFUL!**

WHAT ARE **CATS** GOOD FOR?

GAAAAHH!

COMEDY!

YOU'RE A RIOT.

SPROOINNGG...

ZOIN NNG!

WHAM!

COULDN'T YOU JUST GRAB THE FRISBEE FROM THE TOP OF THE LADDER?

THIS WAY IS MORE FUN.

AH! THE THREE STOOGES!

OOH! THIS IS A GOOD ONE!

✳SIGH...✳

WHAT?

NOTHING.

YOU DON'T **LIKE** THE THREE STOOGES?

HEY, WHAT'S NOT TO LIKE?

PEOPLE FALLING DOWN... SLAPPING EACH OTHER... GETTING HIT WITH PIES...

IT'S **SLAP-STICK!**

WELL, **I** THINK IT'S **CRUEL!**

BUT, HEY! IF YOU GUYS ENJOY LAUGHING AT PEOPLE GETTING **HURT**, WELL, THEN...

...GO RIGHT **AHEAD!**

!

ZZZINNNG!

A CLASSIC!

TIMELESS!

CLAP CLAP CLAP

CLAP CLAP CLAP CLAP

138

HALLO, NATE.

ARTUR, MY MAN!

I'M SELLING CALENDARS FOR MY SCOUT TROOP! CARE TO BUY ONE FOR TWO BUCKS?

TWO DOLLARS? IS GOOD PRICE, YES?

YOU'RE DARN **RIGHT!** ROCK-BOTTOM!

HOKAY. I WILL BUY ONE.

EXCELLENT DECISION, ARTUR! HERE YOU GO!

UH... NATE! EXCUSE, PLEASE.

CALENDAR IS FOR YEAR **2001!**

RIGHT! WHY DO YOU THINK IT ONLY COST TWO BUCKS?! ☆CHUCKLE!☆

HERE'S A LITTLE SAYING YOU SHOULD KEEP IN MIND, ARTUR: "LET THE BUYER BEWARE"!

ALSO IS **ANOTHER** SAYING I AM KEEPING IN MIND:

"SIC 'IM"!

Can YOU tell the difference between an **OLD TEACHER** and a **YOUNG TEACHER?** *here are some* TIPS!

OLD TEACHER: Spends every free moment in the faculty lounge!

Mr. Galvin! I need help with my homework! Mr. Galvin?

knock knock

YOUNG TEACHER: Prefers to be "accessible" to the students!

... Yes, but on page 785 of "Harry Potter and the Order of the Phoenix," I noticed that...

OLD TEACHER: textbook!

Read Chapter 12, answer the questions at the end, then sit quietly until the bell rings.

YOUNG TEACHER: multimedia!

... and after we finish our papier-mâché puppets, there's a **REALLY** cool website I want to show you!

OLD TEACHER: Will NOT deviate from lesson plan... **NO MATTER WHAT!**

I'm confused. Can you explain Question #4?

No, I'm afraid not. There's no time for that.

Moving on to Question #5...

YOUNG TEACHER: Likes to remain "flexible" in the classroom!

Can we watch a video?

I hadn't planned on it, but... **SURE!**

Which video? Suggestions, people?

OLD TEACHER: Has eerie, all-seeing, all-knowing radar!

Stop it.

Stop what?

You know what.

Dang!

YOUNG TEACHER: Has no clue that you're busting on him!

Hey, gang! Who wants a snack?

✷AHEM!✷

OKAY, MEN, THIS IS WHAT WE'VE BEEN WAITING FOR! FIRST GAME OF THE SEASON!

PLAY HARD... PLAY FAIR... AND HAVE FUN!

ANYONE GOT SOMETHING TO ADD BEFORE WE GO OUT THERE?

I DO, COACH!

OKAY, NATE!

JUST ONE SEC!

HONK! BLAAAT!! WONNNK!

BLEEAT! HONNK! BLAAAT!

YOU HAVEN'T TRULY EXPERIENCED MIDDLE SCHOOL ATHLETICS UNTIL YOU'VE HEARD "WE WILL ROCK YOU" PLAYED ON THE TROMBONE.

HEY!

JENNY, M'LADY!

OH, NO...

NATE WRIGHT, ACE REPORTER, AT YOUR SERVICE!

I'M DOING SOME FACT-FINDING FOR MY NEXT "CLASSROOM CHATTERS"!

AH. YOUR IDIOTIC GOSSIP COLUMN.

I'M DOING A "ROMANCE UPDATE"! YOU KNOW, WHO'S GOING STEADY, WHO'S BREAKING UP, STUFF LIKE THAT!

HOW ARE YOU AND RONNIE DOING? A, B, C, OR D?

"A." WE'RE DEFINITELY AN "A".

SO THAT'S "A: STRUGGLING." THANKS, JENNY.

WHOA! WHOA! I THOUGHT YOU MEANT "A" LIKE A GRADE!

NOPE. IT'S MULTIPLE CHOICE. "A" IS "STRUGGLING."

WELL, THEN I WANT TO CHANGE MY ANSWER!

OKAY, ARE YOU GOING WITH B: DOOMED, C: PUTRID, OR D: WILDLY DYSFUNCTIONAL?

THOSE ARE ALL WORSE THAN "A"!!

"A" IT IS, THEN!

WITH A TEMPER LIKE THAT, IT'S NO WONDER THEY'RE STRUGGLING.

I'LL PAY YOU FOUR DOLLARS AN HOUR.

SOUNDS GOOD! THANKS, MR. EUSTIS!

SPITSY, YOU STAY OUT HERE WITH NATE! I'LL BE INSIDE!

WURF!

HEY! SPITSY, **LOOK!** A **CAT!** A **CAT** IN YOUR YARD!

!

NO, NO, **NO!** YOU DON'T **WAG YOUR TAIL** WHEN YOU SEE A **CAT**, YOU IDIOT! A CAT IS YOUR **ARCH ENEMY!**

YES! **THAT'S** MORE LIKE IT! GET TOUGH! GET **NASTY!** SIC 'IM, SPITSY! **SIC 'IM!**

GRRRRRRRR RR

WURF! BARK! BARK! ROWR!

MYOW! WOOF! MWOW! WURF?

YIP! YIP! YIP! YIP!

WOOF

FOR TEN DOLLARS AN HOUR, I'LL MOVE THIS PILE UNDER THE TREE.

I'LL BET MRS. GODFREY READS ME THE RIOT ACT ABOUT NOT GETTING INTO TROUBLE THIS YEAR.

SO TALK TO HER **FIRST!**

TELL HER YOU'RE GOING TO BE A MODEL STUDENT THIS YEAR! FIRE A PRE-EMPTIVE STRIKE!

A PRE-EMPTIVE STRIKE?

A PRE-EMPTIVE STRIKE!

MRS. GODFREY, I JUST WANT YOU TO KNOW THAT THIS YEAR I'M GO—...

NATE, I'M BUSY RIGHT NOW. SIT DOWN, PLEASE.

BUT CAN I JUST TELL YOU THAT I'M...

NATE, DID YOU HEAR WHAT I SAID? SIT **DOWN**, PLEASE!

LOOK, ALL I'M TRYING TO SAY IS...

NATE! I'VE TOLD YOU **TWICE** ALREADY!

NOW, FOR THE **THIRD** TIME... **SIT DOWN!!**

THREE PRE-EMPTIVE STRIKES AND YOU'RE OUT.

WARNING:

The following edition of "CELEBRITY INTERVIEW" may contain disturbing imagery.

Greetings, all! BIFF BIFFWELL here chatting with foliage legend... LEAF ERICKSON!!

How's it going, Leaf?

Well, I'm hangin' in there.

I notice you're the last one left on your tree.

You're darn right! I'm stayin' right here!

Uh... can you do that?

Can, SHMAN! I'm DOIN' it!

You think I want to end up ROTTING on that cold, hard ground? Not ME, friend! NO WAY!

But... the WIND!

Wind?

NO!... NO!!

PLEASE! NO!

FWIK!

Leaf?

Yo.

154

YES? / HI, LADY! I'M SELLING WRAPPING PAPER FOR MY SCOUT TROOP AND...

WAIT! HOLD IT RIGHT THERE!

HMM?

I CAN'T **DO** THIS ANYMORE! I **CAN'T** BUY ANY MORE **STUFF!**

I'VE BOUGHT COOKIES TO SUPPORT THE GIRL SCOUTS, CANDLES TO SUPPORT THE MARCHING BAND, CALENDARS TO SUPPORT THE SWIM TEAM...

I'VE BOUGHT STUFFED ANIMALS FROM THE LATIN CLUB, COFFEE MUGS FROM THE MATH TEAM, AND PICTURE FRAMES FROM THE YEARBOOK COMMITTEE!

MY HOUSE IS FILLED WITH **JUNK!** I CAN'T **TAKE** IT ANYMORE!

WHY NOT GIVE SOME OF IT AWAY AS GIFTS?

...AND TO DO **THAT**, YOU'LL NEED SOME OF THIS FABULOUS **WRAPPING PAPER!**

SHE GAVE ME FIVE BUCKS JUST TO GO AWAY!

HI, MRS. SHIPULSKI.

HELLO, NATE.

I'M HERE TO SEE PRINCIPAL NICHOLS.

YOU'LL HAVE TO WAIT. ARTUR IS IN WITH HIM RIGHT NOW.

!! ARTUR !!

MM-HM. HAVE A SEAT.

WELL, **WELL!** WHO WOULD'VE **THUNK** IT!

AR**TUR** IS IN THE **PRINCIPAL'S** OFFICE! I GUESS **MR. PERFECT** MUST HAVE **SCREWED UP!**

PRETTY **QUIET** IN THERE!

☆CHUCKLE!☆ ARTUR MUST BE SQUIRMING IN HIS SEAT WHILE NICHOLS GIVES HIM THE **HAIRY EYEBALL!**

WONDERFUL JOB, ARTUR! IT'S BEEN **THIRTY YEARS** SINCE ONE OF OUR STUDENTS EARNED THE CITYWIDE "GOOD CITIZENSHIP" AWARD!

YOU'VE MADE US VERY PROUD, SON!

WE'LL PUT YOUR PLAQUE IN THE DISPLAY CASE IMMEDIATELY!

THANK YOU, SIR.

OH, HOW I HATE HIM.

NEXT?

WRIGHT!

YIP!

WHAT'S THE HOLD-UP HERE? THE SCRIMMAGE IS STARTING! EVERYBODY'S WAITING!!

I CAN'T FIND MY MOUTHGUARD.

AGAIN? WHAT'S THAT, THE TENTH TIME TODAY?

IT WAS HERE A SECOND AGO.

IS THIS IT?

YEAH! YEAH, THAT'S IT!

WELL, DON'T JUST STAND THERE! PUT IT IN!!

NMPH!

NOW GET OUT THERE!! TIME'S A-WASTING! GO! GO! GO!

WUMP!

PTOO!

? ? ?

I CAN'T FIND MY MOUTHGUARD.

WHAT'RE YOU READING?

"GARFIELD." ...WHO, BY THE WAY, IS A **CAT**!

SO?

SO, THERE ARE A LOT MORE **CATS** IN CARTOONS AND COMICS THAN **DOGS**, I'LL BET!

I THINK NOT.

HEATHCLIFF! KRAZY KAT! FLESHY! TOM!

SNOOPY! DROOPY! GOOFY! MARMADUKE! DOGBERT!

BUCKY KATT! TOP CAT! FELIX THE CAT! CATBERT!

OFFISSA PUP! DEPUTY DAWG! SCOOBY DOO! PLUTO! ASTRO! OTTO!

BILL THE CAT! SYLVESTER THE CAT!

JOSIE AND THE PUSSYCATS! THE **ARISTOCATS**!

UH... OK... UMM.... LET'S SEE HERE...

RUFF!

YES!... **YES**!! DENNIS THE MENACE'S DOG IS NAMED **RUFF**! **HA!**

WAY TO GO, SPITSY!

DOGGONE IT.

NATE!

HM?

MAYBE YOU COULD STOP PLAYING **TABLE FOOTBALL** AND WORK ON OUR **REPORT**, FOOL!

DON'T CALL ME "FOOL", GINA! I'M NOT A FOOL!

ASK ANYONE! ASK THE TEACHERS! ASK THE GUIDANCE COUNSELOR!

THEY ALL SAY THE SAME THING: I'VE GOT UN-LIMITED POTENTIAL AND COULD DO OUTSTANDING WORK IF I APPLIED MYSELF!

THEY WOULDN'T WASTE THEIR TIME TELLING ME TO DO BETTER IF THEY DIDN'T THINK I **COULD**!

IN OTHER WORDS, YOU'RE A DISAPPOINTMENT TO EVERYONE.

EXACTLY! THAT **PROVES** HOW SMART I AM!

MY HEAD HURTS.

YOU'RE PROBABLY WORKING TOO HARD.

HERE COMES MY PET PROJECT!

CHESTER?

CHESTER IS YOUR PET PROJECT?

THAT'S RIGHT! I'M GOING TO REFORM HIM!

REFORM HIM? WHY?

LOOK, EVERYONE'S AFRAID OF THE GUY, RIGHT?

...BUT HE MUST HAVE SOME GOOD IN HIM! NOBODY'S BORN THAT MEAN!

HE ACTS LIKE A BULLY BECAUSE NOBODY'S EVER BEEN NICE TO HIM! IF I TREAT HIM LIKE A FRIEND, HE'LL STOP BEING SUCH A THUG!

IT SAYS SO RIGHT HERE IN THIS BOOK!

PAT PAT

CHESTER, MY MAN!

W H A M !

"UNDERSTANDING BULLIES"

HE'S A WORK IN PROGRESS.

Peirce

The GAME FACE

POW!

GREETINGS, LADY! I'M SELLING NEEDLEPOINT WALL HANGINGS TO RAISE MONEY FOR MY JUNIOR WOODCHUCK TROOP!

SEE? IT'S GOT A FAMILIAR SAYING AT THE TOP, SOME FLOWERS AT THE BOTTOM... AND IT'S ONLY TEN DOLLARS!

IT LOOKS A LITTLE FRAYED THERE

YEAH, THAT HAPPENS ALL THE TIME. THEY START TO UNRAVEL.

WHAT WILL YOUR TROOP DO WITH THE MONEY?

BEATS ME. PROBABLY BUY SOME LAME SAFETY PAMPHLETS OR SOMETHING.

WELL, WHAT OTHER ONES DO YOU HAVE?

THIS IS THE ONLY ONE I'VE GOT LEFT.

FOR TEN DOLLARS I DON'T EVEN GET A CHOICE?

YEAH, YOU'RE RIGHT. THIS THING'S NOT WORTH TEN CENTS, LET ALONE TEN BUCKS.

BUT HEY, IT'S FOR A GOOD CAUSE, RIGHT? AND YOU LOOK PRETTY RICH!

SLAM!

HA!

Honesty is the Best Policy

SAME OLD SAME OLD.

WHAT DO YOU MEAN?

ALL YOU EVER DRAW IS MEAN CARTOONS ABOUT OUR TEACHERS!

HEE HEE! YEAH, I KNOW! IT'S MY SPECIALTY!

CARTOONS DON'T HAVE TO BE **CRUEL** ALL THE TIME! TRY DRAWING A **NICE** CARTOON ABOUT A TEACHER!

A NICE CARTOON?

OKAY, I ACCEPT YOUR CHALLENGE! I'LL DRAW A NICE CARTOON ABOUT MRS. GODFREY!

I CAN DO THIS.

I... CAN... ✲GASP!✲ DO...THIS... I... I...

BWA HA HA HA HA

YOU CALL THAT **NICE?**

I **MEANT** IT TO BE! I WAS **THINKING** NICE, BUT THEN MY DRAWING HAND TOOK OVER!

MY MIND WAS STRONG, BUT MY FLESH WAS WEAK!

YOU'RE HALF RIGHT.

!

Time for **BIFF** and **CHIP**.... **ON SAFARI!**

G'day, mates!

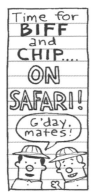

In Nature, Chip, "OPPOSITES ATTRACT"!

Right, Biff! Let's take a look at the unlikely friendship...

...between the lumbering 6th grade Social Studies teacher...

Or, in scientific jargon, "Bad Breathius Hideosa".

...AND the hyperactive, eager-to-please TEACHER'S PET!

"Boot-Lickius Obedientius".

What makes this bizarre relationship **WORK**, Chip?

Biff, each of these creatures plays its role **PERFECTLY!**

The TEACHER is a sluggish creature whose instinct is to do NOTHING!

...while the PET lives to do her **BIDDING!**

Shoo, fly!

When she needs something done, he **DOES** it! When she needs something fetched, he **FETCHES** it!

LOOK at her! She barely has to **MOVE!**

But WHY does the pet **STAY** in such a one-sided relationship?

Indeed, Biff: what's in it for HIM?

YOU MAKE ME SICK.

COLONIAL TIME L

OKAY, I'M DONE WITH THE MULTIPLE CHOICE SECTION...

A...B...C...D...A...B... C...D...A...B...C...D... **WAIT** A MINUTE!

MY ANSWERS ARE IN **PERFECT ALPHABETICAL ORDER!** THAT CAN'T BE RIGHT!

MRS. GODFREY WOULD NEVER ARRANGE A TEST LIKE THAT! **NO** TEACHER WOULD!

MULTIPLE CHOICE TESTS ALWAYS HAVE A CERTAIN **LOGICAL RANDOMNESS** TO THEM!

I'LL CHANGE A FEW ANSWERS!

A...C...D...D...B...C... B...A...B...D...C...A

PERFECT! IT'S RANDOM, BUT IT'S NOT **TOO** RANDOM!

K R RI NNG

HAND 'EM IN... HAND 'EM IN...

MRS. GODFREY? WHAT WERE THE ANSWERS TO THE MULTI- PLE CHOICE SECTION?

A, B, C, D, A, B, C, D, A, B, C, D.

SHE'S AN EVIL, EVIL WOMAN.

YESSSS! I GOT A HUNDRED AND FIVE ON THE TEST!

A HUNDRED AND **FIVE**??

GINA, YOU CAN'T GET HIGHER THAN A HUNDRED!

WELL, **I** DID! HERE'S WHAT HAPPENED:

DURING THE TEST, I NOTICED THAT MRS. GODFREY HAD MADE A TYPOGRAPHICAL ERROR ON QUESTION SIX!

I CORRECTED HER MISTAKE, AND SHE GAVE ME FIVE POINTS EXTRA CREDIT!

HMMM

SO IF **I** NOTICE A MISTAKE THAT MRS. GODFREY MADE, MAYBE **I'LL** GET EXTRA CREDIT!

MAYBE! WORKED FOR ME!

MRS. GODFREY?

MMM?

BOY, DID YOU EVER SCREW UP ON QUESTION EIGHT! LET ME SHOW YOU...

FOR YOU, SHE GIVETH. FOR ME, SHE TAKETH AWAY.

WELCOME PLAYERS! TRI-COUNTY SCHOLASTIC **CHESS** TOURNAMENT — REGISTER HERE →

HOW'RE YOU DOING SO FAR?

I WON MY FIRST MATCH!

PAT?

PAT BLEVINS OF AMESBURY MIDDLE SCHOOL VERSUS NATE WRIGHT OF P.S. 38!

HMM...THIS GUY DOESN'T LOOK TOO TOUGH!

STILL, HE'S IN THE WINNER'S BRACKET, SO MAYBE HE'S... HMM? HE'S **WHISTLING!**

WELL, EITHER HE'S NOT TAKING THE MATCH SERIOUSLY, OR... ?? WHA-?... NOW HE'S EATING **CHEEZ DOODLES!**

CRUNCH MUNCH

...AND WHAT SORT OF WEIRD MOVE IS **THAT**?... DOES THIS KID HAVE ANY IDEA WHAT HE'S **DOING**?

!! NOW I'VE SEEN **EVERYTHING!** HE'S READING A **COMIC BOOK!**

THIS KID'S **CLUELESS!** I'M GONNA BLOW HIM OFF THE BOARD!

HELLO? IS HE GOING TO **DO** SOMETHING? DOES HE EVEN **KNOW** IT'S **HIS MOVE?**

CHECKMATE

!

HOW'RE YOU DOING SO FAR?

OH, SHUT UP.

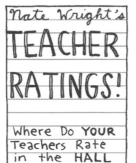
Nate Wright's

TEACHER RATINGS!

Where Do **YOUR** Teachers Rate in the HALL OF SHAME?

NOTE: Ratings are based on a scale of **zero** (worst) to **ten** (best)

MR. STAPLES (Math)

"< fun"

Today, the fascinating world of... FRACTIONS!

RATING: 2.0

MRS. BRINDLE (LIFE SKILLS)

"A recipe for disaster"

...and after 20 minutes, our "johnny-cake" is done!

RATING: 1.3

MS. LA CHANCE (French)

"Ooh La Loser"

Let the words RRRRROLL off your tongue!

RATING: 0.8

MR. GALVIN (Science)

"Boredom = mc²"

You don't know what I'm saying, do you? Well, I don't know what I'm saying either.

RATING: 1.4

MR. ALDRIDGE (Computer Lab)

Press "escape"

Wait. Wait. That wasn't supposed to... Okay, wait. Wait.

tik tak tik tak tik tak

RATING: 1.1

MRS. GODFREY (Social Studies)

"Oh, the humanity."

I summon thee, hounds of Satan!

RATING: -3,000,000

DO YOU ACTUALLY EXPECT ME TO PUT THIS IN THE DISPLAY CASE?

THINK OF IT AS A PUBLIC SERVICE!

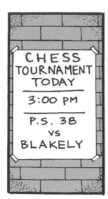

CHESS
TOURNAMENT
TODAY

3:00 PM

P.S. 38
vs
BLAKELY

WHAT A REVOLTING DEVELOPMENT! HERE I SIT, PLAYING AGAINST THEIR SECOND-BEST PLAYER!

...WHILE ARTUR GETS TO PLAY AGAINST THEIR NUMBER ONE!

THAT SHOULD BE ME OVER THERE.

BEFORE "CHESS BOY" CAME ALONG, I WAS OUR TEAM'S TOP PLAYER!

BUT... WAIT A SEC! WHAT IF ARTUR LOSES?

IF ARTUR LOSES HIS MATCH AND I WIN MINE, I'LL BE BACK ON TOP! I'LL BE NUMBER ONE!

SOUNDS LIKE A PLAN! I'LL JUST POLISH THIS GUY OFF AND...

CHECKMATE

CHECKMATE

GET
SMART.

PLAY
CHESS.

VERY FUNNY.

I'VE GOT A "GRAND CANYON" CALENDAR... A "LOVE THOSE CATS" CALENDAR...

HMM... WELL, I'M NOT SURE...

HOW ABOUT A SIERRA CLUB CALENDAR? OR "PRECIOUS PUPPIES"?

I JUST DON'T THINK...

IT'S FOR THE CAMP-SITE GIRLS! IT'S A GOOD CAUSE!

OH, ALL RIGHT... I SUPPOSE I'LL TAKE...

I'LL TAKE THE PUPPIES ONE.

GOOD CHOICE!

OR...

OR?

"CHIPPEN-DALES® 2004: HOT 'N BEEFY"!

SOLD!

!

IN DOOR-TO-DOOR SALES, INVENTORY IS EVERYTHING!

LET'S TOSS AROUND THE PIGSKIN, NATE!

GROANN...

OH, COME ON! IT'LL BE FUN! I'LL BE THE QUARTERBACK, YOU GO OUT FOR THE PASS!

SIGHHH...

OKAY, HERE'S MY PATTERN:

I'LL RUN TO THE PINE TREE, THEN SLANT BACK TO THE DRIVE-WAY.

THEN I'LL CUT BACK TO THE FENCE, ACROSS THE STREET TO THE STORM DRAIN, AND DOWN TO THE END OF THE BLOCK.

FROM THERE, I'LL HEAD OVER TO BENSON STREET, TAKE THE SHORTCUT THROUGH THE PARK, AND END UP AT TEDDY'S HOUSE.

I'LL ZIG ACROSS HIS LIVING ROOM, ZAG ONTO HIS COUCH, AND HANG OUT THERE FOR A COUPLE HOURS.

READY... **HIKE!**

LUCKILY, MY DAD'S NOT AT ALL ATHLETIC.

NEITHER IS MINE. THAT'S WHY I'M HERE.

Tired of the same old superheroes? Meet...

SUPERDAD!

... the world's **ONLY** bald superhero with a slight paunch!

FASTER than the average 46-year-old!...

GASP!

PANT! HEAVE!

Mommy, is that man having a heart attack?

STRONGER than a jar of sweet mini gherkins!...

YES! **GOT** it!

Now that's **MUSCLE**!

But you used vise grips!

MORE POWERFUL than... than... uh... well, we'll come back to that one.

ZZZZZZZONK!

Able to **LEAP** to conclusions in a single bound!

Who ate the last doughnut? It was **YOU**, wasn't it, **NATE**?

Yes, he's **SUPER-DAD!!** Defender of the defenseless! Protector of the weak! Fearless guardian of the...

DING DONG!

YOU answer that.

HI, THERE! MAY I SPEAK TO THE HEAD OF THE HOUSEHOLD ABOUT VINYL SIDING?

I'M NOT HERE.

NATE!

HUH?

HAVE YOU EVER HEARD OF A LITTLE SOMETHING CALLED **BODY LANGUAGE**?

UH...I GUESS SO.

WELL, **YOURS** IS **AWFUL**! YOU'RE **SLOUCHING**! YOU'RE ALL **SLUMPED OVER**!

A STUDENT IN **MY** CLASS NEEDS TO LOOK **ALERT**! YOU NEED TO SHOW ME YOU'RE **READY TO LEARN**!

PSST! NATE! I CAN HELP YOU WITH THAT!

HMM?

YANK!

NOW **THAT'S** MORE **LIKE** IT!

BEHOLD THE POWER OF THE WEDGIE.

TEDDY! DID YOU DO THE HOMEWORK FOR MRS. PINHEAD?

MRS. PINHEAD?

ULP!... I... HEH HEH!... I MEANT "MRS. PINFOLD."

I KNOW WHAT YOU **MEANT**, NATE! I'M SURE **ALL** THE TEACHERS HAVE LITTLE NICKNAMES, MY**SELF** INCLUDED!

Y-YOU? ☆CHOKE!☆ OH NO, THAT'S NOT...

I CAN TAKE IT, NATE. TELL ME: WHAT DO THE STUDENTS CALL **ME**?

UH... WELL... W-WON'T YOU GET MAD?

I PROMISE I WON'T GET MAD.

OKAY, THERE'S.... GODZILLA, GOD-AWFUL, JABBA THE HUTT, EXTRA CHEESE, DRAGON BREATH, THIGH MASTER, BLACK WIDOW, CLARABELL...

SHE-WHO-MUST-NOT-BE-NAMED, WIDE LOAD, FAT CITY, HELMET HEAD, ONE-TON SOUP, PUDGE, FREE WILLY, BOREDOM.COM...

I CAN'T BELIEVE SHE'S NOT BUTTER, HEIDI HO-HO, LASSIE, CHINS-R-US...

ENOUGH!

BROKE HER PROMISE!

TOUCHY.

HERE, SHOOT SOME VIDEO OF MY HOME-WORK.

YOUR HOME-WORK?

I CAN NEVER GET MY HOMEWORK TO SCHOOL WITHOUT IT GETTING **RUINED** SOMEHOW!

THIS WAY I'LL HAVE PHOTO DOCUMENTATION THAT I **DID** THE ASSIGNMENT, NO MATTER **WHAT** HAPPENS!

ZOOM IN! GET A CLOSE-UP!

BZZZZZZZZ

OW!

BZZZAP!

SPLOOSH!

NO!

SHLOOOOP!

NOT TO WORRY! I GOT IT ALL ON TAPE!

BOBO! COME BACK!

BOBO!

GRAB!

STOMP! STOMP! STOMP! STOMP! STOMP!

BAD BOBO! BAD!

... SO THEN ®CHIMPANZEE STOMPED ON ©VIDEOTAPE...

SIGH...

UH... LOOK HERE, YOUNG FELLER...

HOWDY, EMMITT!

I'VE GOT TO MOP THIS HALLWAY. YOU'LL HAVE TO THROW AWAY ALL THIS TRASH.

TRASH? THIS ISN'T TRASH!

LOOKS LIKE TRASH.

ONE MAN'S TRASH IS ANOTHER MAN'S TREASURE!

WHATEVER. THROW IT AWAY.

BUT THERE'S A LOT OF GOOD STUFF IN HERE!

LIKE WHAT?

NAME IT! I CAN FIND ANYTHING IN HERE!

ANYTHING, EH?

ANYTHING!

✳CHUCKLE!✳ CAN YOU FIND A COPY OF ARTHUR "GUITAR BOOGIE" SMITH'S RECORDING OF "WHO SHOT WILLIE"?

RUSTLE
RUSTLE
RUSTLE

78 OR 45?

GAWK!

HE DOUBTED ME!

WHAT'S WITH THE FRISBEES?

TIME! GAME OVER, GENTS!

HONK

WHAT'S WITH YOU?

WHATTA YA MEAN?

WHY DO YOU LOOK SO MAD?

WE WON!

I KNOW.

BUT I'VE STILL GOT MY GAME FACE ON!

I SPENT ALL DAY GETTING PSYCHED UP FOR THIS GAME! I WILLED MY FACE INTO A MASK OF COMPETITIVE INTENSITY!

I CAN'T JUST TURN OFF THAT INTENSITY LIKE A...

HELLO, LADIES!

...LIKE A HOSE.

WHATCHA GOT?

AN OLD YEARBOOK!

OVER IN THE REFERENCE STACKS THEY HAVE COPIES OF EVERY YEARBOOK IN THE SCHOOL'S HISTORY!

COOL!

THIS ONE'S FROM TWENTY YEARS AGO! IT'S TOTALLY HILARIOUS!

QUIET PLEASE

IS THAT... MR. GALVIN?

HEE HEE! YUP! HE WAS ACTUALLY YOUNG ONCE!

WOW! LOOK AT MRS. BELLAMY!

✷ SNICKER! ✷ TWENTY YEARS AND FORTY POUNDS AGO!

QU PLE

HEY! IS MR. ROSA IN THERE?

LET'S SEE...

FLIP FLIP

MMPH! NICE HAIR!

✷ SNORT! ✷ NICE DISCO SHIRT!

HA HA HA

HA HEE HEE

HA HA

HELLO, BOYS.

WA HA HA HA HA HA HA HA HA HA

THIS IS WHY, DURING FREE PERIODS, I TEND TO STAY IN MY CLASSROOM WITH THE DOOR LOCKED.

HA HA HA HA HA

HE'S A DISCO INFERNO!

HA HA HA HA

G is for the Gruesome class she teaches;

O is for Obese, it's plain to see.

D is for her favorite Dinner: leeches.

F, the grade she gives most Frequently.

R is for her Rages never-ending;

E, her Evil Eye which never blinks.

Y is for my Youth which I am spending

sitting in detention.

MAN, THIS STINKS.

LOTS OF PEOPLE HERE TODAY. THIS IS THE BIGGEST CROWD WE'VE HAD ALL YEAR!

WELL, THEY'RE NOT GONNA SEE ANYONE SCORE ON **ME**, I'LL GUARANT—...✳

OOP! LOOK WHO'S HERE! **JENNY!**

...AND LOOK WHO **ELSE! GREG PROXMIRE!** HER **MAIN SQUEEZE!**

I CAN'T **BELIEVE** THEY'RE STILL AN ITEM! THE QUESTION IS: **WHY?**

I MEAN, WHAT'S THE APPEAL? HE'S A **STIFF!** SHE COULD DO SO MUCH BETTER!

LIKE **ME**, FOR INSTANCE! DOESN'T SHE REALIZE I'M **PERFECT** FOR HER? DOESN'T SHE...

✳AHEM!✳

WHAT'S YOUR PROBLEM?

MY PROBLEM? **GREG PROXMIRE**, THAT'S MY PROBLEM!

WHAT'S **HE** GOT THAT **I** HAVEN'T GOT?

WELL, FOR ONE THING, HE'S MORE OBSERVANT.

IN WHAT WAY?

CRIPES.

HEY, **DWEEB!**

UH OH! IT'S JOSH PANKIN!

YOU'RE IN **TROUBLE**, FRANCIS!

ME? WHAT DID **I** DO?

YOU COVERED UP YOUR PAPER DURING THE TEST SO I COULDN'T COPY OFF YOU! I PROBABLY **FLUNKED** THANKS TO YOU!

THAT'S GONNA COST YOU SOME **COIN**, PINHEAD!

B-BUT I DON'T HAVE ANY MONEY!

HOLD IT, **HOLD** IT!

SETTLE DOWN, JOSH! I'M SURE FRANCIS AND I HAVE SOME CASH IN OUR LOCKER!

RIGHT THIS WAY.

FOOM!

I'LL NEVER CRITICIZE YOU AGAIN FOR BEING A SLOB!

YOU'RE WELCOME!

Time Again For... **UP CLOSE** and **PERSONAL**

Your Host: BIFF BIFFWELL!

Today's special guest is Halloween pumpkin **JACK O'LANTERN!** How's it goin', Jack?

Not good, Biff.

Why not?

Why **NOT**? I'll **TELL** you why not!

One minute I'm sitting in my patch, minding my own business... the **NEXT** minute I'm lying on a bunch of **NEWSPAPERS** in somebody's **kitchen!!**

Can you imagine my **shock** when all of a sudden, somebody started cutting me up with a **KNIFE**?!

Wow.

Wow **INDEED!** Before I knew what was going on, I'd been **DISEMBOWELED!**

So you're not happy about becoming a Halloween pumpkin?

HAPPY?! Do I **LOOK** happy?

Well... Yes!

Go ahead, make jokes. I'm spilling my guts here.

Time Once Again For...
Celebrity
INTERVIEW!!

Here's your host:
CHIP CHIPSON!

Greetings, friends! I'm joined today by "osteo-activist" **WILLIE WISHBONE!**

Yo, Chip.

Now, Willie... it says in your press release that you "fight for the rights of bones."

Darn right.

Think of what we bones have to **GO** through! We get boiled in soup... we get chewed on by dogs...

...and **WORST** of all is what happened to **ME**! **NO** bone should have to go through such an ordeal!

They took me out of the turkey, cleaned me off, dried me out for a couple days... and then gave me to some **KIDS!**

Those little monsters pulled on my legs for what seemed like **HOURS**! I just couldn't **TAKE** it anymore!!

And then?...

I just snapped.

HI, MR. EUSTIS! CAN N.F.T. YARD-CARE RAKE YOUR LEAVES?

NOT THIS YEAR, NATE. I NEED THE EXERCISE!

HMM... DO YOU REALLY THINK THAT'S WISE?

WHAT DO YOU MEAN?

RAKING LEAVES IS HARD WORK, MR. EUSTIS! REAL CARDIO-VASCULAR STUFF!

AFTER AN HOUR OR TWO, YOU'LL BE PERSPIRING... SHORT OF BREATH... YOUR CHEST AND ARMS WILL FEEL TIGHT...

...AND SUDDENLY, YOU'LL FIND YOURSELF WONDERING: AM I HAVING A HEART ATTACK?

...SO YOU'LL CALL YOUR DOCTOR, WHO WILL CHECK YOU INTO THE HOSPITAL FOR A COMPLETE BATTERY OF TESTS!

TOTAL COST TO YOU: TWELVE, THIRTEEN HUNDRED DOLLARS!

...OR, YOU CAN JUST HIRE US FOR FIFTY!

NICE SALES PITCH!

JUST A BUSINESSMAN DOING MY JOB!

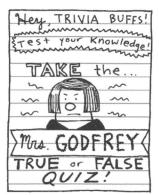
Hey, TRIVIA BUFFS! Test your knowledge! TAKE the... Mrs. GODFREY TRUE or FALSE QUIZ!

TRUE or FALSE: In her high school yearbook, Mrs. Godfrey listed her "hobbies" as "unprovoked rage" and "lunch."

What are YOU lookin' at? HUH?

TRUE or FALSE: At their wedding, Mrs. Godfrey insisted her husband promise to "love, honor, and cower in fear."

Whatever you say, dear!

TRUE or FALSE: In "The Two Towers", Mrs. Godfrey makes a cameo appearance as "Orc #3."

AAARRGHHH

Gandalf! HELP!

TRUE or FALSE: Mrs. Godfrey's breath has been classified as a "weapon of mass destruction."

tuna meat loaf cheese cabbage mold rotten eggs

TRUE or FALSE: To pay for college, Mrs. Godfrey worked part-time as a Slim-Fast "before" model.

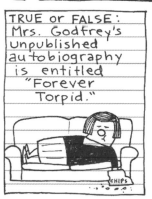
TRUE or FALSE: Mrs. Godfrey's unpublished autobiography is entitled "Forever Torpid."

CHIPS

CHECK IT OUT! TRUE OR FALSE?

! !

TRUE. SO TRUE. AGAIN?

DETENTION

Peirce

207

SHLOX-TV presents:

:25

25 minutes of 6th-grade Social Studies!

Events occur in real time

8:30

Goooood morning, Mrs. Godfrey!

Shut up and sit down.

8:32

Surprise quiz, people.

But... you said we were watching a filmstrip!

Hence the term "surprise" quiz.

8:37

Um... this quiz is on stuff we haven't even studied yet.

Well, you should have read ahead.

8:42

Hand 'em in.

But... I'm only half done!

Ask me if I half-care.

8:44

Okay, now I'm going to drone on and on in a mind-numbing monotone about an obscure and meaningless historical event.

On March 1st, 1790, Congress authorized a decennial U.S. census, meaning that the

8:49 and it was at that point, in 1795, that the U.S. decided to purchase peace from the Algerian pirates who were holding 115 sailors hostage, and follow this

8:53

Are you chewing GUM?

It's a cough drop. I have a cold.

Gum-chewing in class is FORBIDDEN!

8:54

But it isn't gum! It's...

Are you SASSING me, Mister?

No, I...

NO ONE SASSES ME!

PRINCIPAL

TICK TICK TICK TICK

Peirce

WHEW!

THAT SNOW IS **HEAVY!**

YOU SHOVELED?

OF **COURSE** I SHOVELED! I WANTED TO GET IT CLEARED OFF RIGHT AWAY!

WOW!

WHAT A SURPRISE! THAT'S VERY THOUGHTFUL OF YOU, NATE!

I APPRECIATE YOUR HARD WORK! SHOVELING THE DRIVEWAY IS A BIG JOB!

DRIVEWAY?

WHY THE HECK WOULD I SHOVEL THE **DRIVE**WAY?

I SHOVELED THE **POND!**

PRIORITIES, DAD! PRIORITIES!

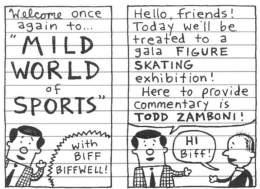

Welcome once again to... "MILD WORLD of SPORTS" with BIFF BIFFWELL!

Hello, friends! Today we'll be treated to a gala FIGURE SKATING exhibition! Here to provide commentary is TODD ZAMBONI!

HI Biff!

Todd, who's our first skater?

It's ELLEN WRIGHT, unveiling a new program!

CLAP! CLAP! CLAP! CLAP! CLAP! CLAP!

...And here comes her first jump!

She INVENTED that move! It's called the "ugly duckling"!

And now... a combination jump!

Yes, it's a combination of CLUMSINESS and INEPTITUDE!

WOW, Todd! What choreography!

I agree, Biff! WHAT choreography??

Like all good routines, this one tells a STORY!

Right, Biff! It's the story of an awkward girl who can't skate very well!

I must say, Todd, Ellen has some UNUSUAL moves!

She sure does! There's no telling what she'll do NEXT!

THAT'S A MOVE I'VE NEVER SEEN BEFORE

DAD, IT'S **FREEZING** OUT HERE!

IT'S **BRISK**, THAT'S ALL! WE CAN'T LET **THAT** STOP US!

WE HAVE A FAMILY FOOTBALL GAME **EVERY** THANKSGIVING WEEKEND! IT'S **TRADITIONAL!**

TRADITIONS ARE IMPORTANT, SON! DOING THE SAME THINGS, IN THE SAME WAY, YEAR AFTER YEAR...THAT HAS **MEANING!**

BUT THERE'S **ICE** ON THE LAWN!

ICE, SCHMICE! KICK OFF!

DOOF!

LET'S HEAR IT FOR **TRADITION!!**

ZZOOOP!

!

WAM!

YOU'RE HERE EVERY YEAR ABOUT THIS TIME, AREN'T YOU?

EMERG
◄ ADMITTIN
◄ X-RAY
◄ PHYSICAL

Peirce

BEEP
BEEP
BEEP
BOOP
BOOP
BEEP
BEEP

YEAH, IS THIS METEOROLOGIST WINK SUMMERS? YO, WINK. NATE WRIGHT HERE.

WHAT'S UP WITH YOUR **FORECAST**, WINK? YOU SAID WE'D HAVE **BELOW-FREEZING** TEMPERATURES ALL WEEKEND!

INSTEAD, IT'S **40 DEGREES** OUTSIDE, IN CASE YOU DIDN'T KNOW!

WHY AM I UPSET? BECAUSE I WANT TO PLAY **HOCKEY**, THAT'S WHY! AND THE LOCAL **SKATING POND** IS A BIG, WET **PUDDLE**!

THE NEXT TIME YOU PROMISE ME **ICE**, WINK, I WANT TO SEE **ICE**! WHAT DO YOU SAY TO **THAT**?

THAT WAS COLD.

THAT'S THE UGLIEST SNOWMAN I'VE EVER SEEN.

IT'S A SNOW **WOMAN**! IT'S MRS. GODFREY!

! ! MRS. **GOD-FREY**!?

LOOK, TEDDY... TOMORROW SHE GETS BACK FROM HER SABBATICAL, RIGHT?

SHE'LL BE THE ONE WITH ALL THE **POWER**! **SHE'LL** HAVE THE HAMMER!

SO I'M STRIKING BACK IN THE ONLY WAY I CAN! I'VE SCULPTED MRS. GODFREY OUT OF SNOW...

..AND NOW, I'M GOING TO **KNOCK HER DOWN**!

YAAAAAA

WAM!

HOW SYMBOLIC!

OH, HOW I HATE HER.

WHAT'S UP?

I'M RESURFACING THE ICE!

IT'S ALMOST LIKE HAVING A ZAMBONI! JUST TURN ON THE HOSE AND LET IT FREEZE!

IT'S SO COLD OUT TODAY, IT'LL TAKE NO TIME AT ALL!

BIFF BIFFWELL, hard-hitting interviewer, *chats with...* consumer reporter **CELINE PAYCHEK!**

Celine, our mailbag is **FULL** of letters asking: what should I get **DAD** for Christmas... on a **LIMITED BUDGET??**

Good question, Biff!

High-end gifts for Dad, like the "Reach-A-Round Razor" for pesky back hair...

bzzzz

...or the "Snak-o-belt"® are simply too **EXPENSIVE** for most buyers!

Instead, I advise shoppers to **WAIT** until the **LAST MINUTE!** Buy that gift for Dad today or tomorrow, when the prices **DROP!**

So there are bargains to be found, eh?

There sure are, Biff! However, there **IS** a downside!

Most of the **GOOD** merchandise has been picked over! Shopping for Dad at the last minute means you **MIGHT** have **LESS** to **CHOOSE FROM!**

CLEARA

I CAN AFFORD **BOTH** THE COWBOY HAT **AND** THE "BUNS OF STEEL" VIDEO!

HE'LL BE THRILLED.

To Ellen
From Nate

HMM!... WHAT COULD **THIS** BE?

OH, IT... IT'S NOTHING, REALLY.

I COULDN'T FIGURE OUT WHAT TO GET YOU, ELLEN. I WENT INTO A ZILLION DIFFERENT STORES, BUT NOTHING SEEMED RIGHT.

FINALLY, I DECIDED I'D JUST **MAKE** YOU A PRESENT WITH WHATEVER MATERIALS I COULD COME UP WITH.

I CLIPPED STUFF OUT OF YOUR FAVORITE MAGAZINES... FOUND PICTURES OF YOUR FAVORITE SINGERS AND MOVIE STARS... COLLECTED PHOTOS FROM YOUR FRIENDS AND CLASSMATES...

IT TOOK **DAYS**, BUT FINALLY I FINISHED IT! A COLLAGE!...

...A COLLAGE IN THE SHAPE OF YOUR SILHOUETTE.

HOW **SWEET**!

m e r r y
CHRISTMAS!!

★☆★☆★☆★☆

Celebrity INTER-VIEW!

with: BIFF BIFFWELL!

Friends, I'm chatting today with the big fella himself... SANTA CLAUS!

Season's greetings, Biff!

Santa, I've often wondered... what's the most FRUST-RATING part of your job?

These LETTERS, Biff!

Take THIS one, for example: a boy named NATE WRIGHT has asked me to bring him a DOG!

Sounds simple enough!

Not so fast, Biff! Nate's DAD doesn't WANT him to have a dog!.... And I'm not ALLOWED to overrule a PARENT!

That DOES sound frust-rating!

And UNFAIR! Just another case of a parent being SELFISH!

So what do you do? Punish Nate's Dad?

Hey, I'm Santa Claus! It's not in my job description to punish parents!

So instead, I pick up the phone and call my friend MOTHER NATURE!

Mother Nature? What can SHE do?

Peirce

HI, COULD I PLEASE SPEAK TO CHIEF METEOROLOGIST WINK SUMMERS?

WINK? NATE WRIGHT HERE. LISTEN, MY MAN, YOU MISSED THE MARK WITH LAST NIGHT'S FORECAST! **BIG** TIME!

YES, I **KNOW** YOU PREDICTED SNOW, WINK, BUT YOU PREDICTED **FLUFFY** SNOW!

THIS STUFF IS ALL WET AND STICKY!

YOU HAD ME ALL HYPED UP FOR A DAY OF **TUBING**, WINK, BUT I CAN'T TUBE ON **THIS** SLOP!

THE ONLY THING **THIS** SNOW IS GOOD FOR IS...

WINK? I'LL CALL YOU BACK!

POW!